# TRUE FAITH

TRU

FAIT

GARTH ENNIS
WARREN PLEECE

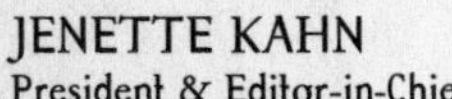

TRUE FAITH
Published by
DC Comics, 1700 Broadway
New York, NY 10019.



DC Comics. A division of Warner Bros. - A Time Warner Entertainment Company. Printed in Canada. First printing.

ISBN: 1-56389-378-9

Publication design by Kim Grzybek

# Introduction
BY GARTH ENNIS

I don't look at my earliest work much, and when I do my reaction is usually, "Oh, Christ."

My second reaction, if I'm feeling charitable, runs something like, "Well, the funny bits are okay, the violent bits are okay, the rest... oh, Christ."

I was given my first professional writing assignment on my nineteenth birthday, a little over eight years ago. Now, eight years may not seem long – certainly not long enough for someone to be banging on about their "earliest work" – but believe you me, sometimes it feels like a lifetime.

Back in January of '89, the job came as a godsend. It helped me to escape from university, provided me with beer vouchers at a rate I'd never experienced before, and it was pure joy: to be paid to make up stories, well, what could be better than that? It also — though I never once stopped to consider this at the time — meant I would be going through the unpleasant business of *growing up in public*.

You can't escape your own work. Most of the time you don't want to, you're perfectly happy with it, but everyone has those ghastly skeletons rattling around in their creative cupboard. "Look," they shout, "look at this bit! Look at that really naff line! That totally implausible character! That whacking great hole in the plot! Writer? More like *Shiter* if you ask me!" (Being creative skeletons, they're not very good at wordplay.) And unlike your wanky teenage poetry, or your appalling short fiction about suicide (not guilty on either count, I'm happy to say), the bastard things are in print. They're available. People can read them. They are the drooling, twitching, idiot children that you tried to disown and drown in a septic tank, and they're coming back to get you.

So what you're probably wondering, having just shelled out the dinero for what you'll be delighted to hear was my second professional assignment, is *Hold on, is he trying to tell me this thing's crap? Have I just wasted good crack money on some load of old bollocks?* Good question, my friend. Read on.

TRUE FAITH first saw print around October of 1989, when it was serialized in the British political anthology *Crisis*. I had previously written *Troubled Souls* for this title, and as that had gone down reasonably well with the readership, the editorial team was willing to trust me a second time. It was my great good fortune to have as my editor Steve MacManus, who, with ten years' experience at the helm of *2000AD* under his belt, was able to keep me more or less on course. He and his then-assistant Peter Hogan gave me the chance to go a little bit nuts and have some more very dark fun, and I would like to express my appreciation for, and gratitude to, both of these gentlemen. Your health, lads.

*Troubled Souls* was set in my native Belfast, a grim tale of bombing and shooting folk that sometimes collapsed under both its own weight and my lack of research. I was determined that TRUE FAITH would be a more personal story, that it would concern itself directly with my own personal obsessions (religious mania, the misuse of power, machine guns), and that it would generally have a lot more jokes in it.

It was Steve MacManus, in fact, who found me the perfect co-conspirator: Mr. Warren Pleece, a mischievous, cynical troublemaker of considerable talent and dubious morality. Along with his even more jaded brother, Gary, Warren had been producing the excellent *Velocity*, which still makes an occasional appearance all these years later. Every issue, the brothers Pleece dissect yet another rotten organ of the decaying England they see outside their window. The family that *sneers* together stays together. Albion in all its crapness lies at their feet. They're obviously having a bloody good laugh, and the art is *great*.

Warren's artwork made my story live and breathe. He understood perfectly the feeling I was trying to capture, and his harsh black lines and gloomy, stained colors created a land we might find vaguely familiar: late twentieth-century London with a (slight) twist. The world of

TRUE FAITH was suddenly real and vivid, the perfect backdrop for a darkly comic tale of fear and madness, of nasty little men with big ideas, of petty lusts and jealousies, and of sudden, all-consuming violence.

Not long after the end of its run in *Crisis*, the decision was made to collect TRUE FAITH in a more durable trade paperback edition. This was duly done, the book being released in late October of 1990. It remained on sale for exactly two months, and was then withdrawn after a series of complaints from churches and religious groups. I suddenly found myself at the center of a brief but vigorous debate on censorship in comics – an odd position to be in, when one is convinced (as I was, and still am) that the furor over TRUE FAITH was simply a massive overreaction on the part of all concerned.

That being said, the essential truth remains that Warren and I had been censored, and very effectively so. The original back issues of *Crisis* were still available if you could find them, copies of the trade paperback surfaced from time to time, but TRUE FAITH had, to all intents and purposes, been cast into publishing limbo. And this miserable state of affairs was to persist for several years afterward.

Enter Ms. Karen Berger, Executive Editor of DC Comics' VERTIGO line. It seems that Karen had been a bit of a TRUE FAITH fan for some time, and it's largely thanks to her efforts that you're holding this volume in your hands today. I'm extremely grateful to her, and – my earlier remarks notwithstanding – very glad to see the reappearance of this bleak little tale. It's clumsy, yes; it's unpolished; it smacks strongly of adolescent wish-fulfillment and I have to admit that I stole the title from a New Order song; but for me, TRUE FAITH was where I began to find my voice. It marks the beginning of a creative path I've been on ever since, a preoccupation with faith and its abuses that has, among other things, led to the creation of my pride and joy, PREACHER. This is either a very good or a very bad thing, depending on your point of view...

Is there a lesson to be learned from all of this? Censorship is wrong? Christianity is stupid? Watch your back? Don't let the bastards get you down, because if you wait long enough a nice lady will come along and reprint your book, and you'll have the last laugh? I don't know; I think lessons are largely personal things. I know what I've learned from the whole affair, but I'm not about to spout out a series of rules that I believe are applicable to any given situation.

Perhaps what we can draw from the TRUE FAITH business is a simple truth: Someone, call them the censors, call them the church, call them a bunch of tits with too much time on their hands, I don't know – but *someone* didn't want you to see this book. And now, thanks to the work of a number of people, you can.

Is it a good book? Well, the funny bits are okay, the violent bits are okay, the rest... you'll have to make your own mind up about that.

Hey, feel free.

Garth Ennis
London, March 1997

EPISODE ONE: THE WARRIORS
12TH SEPTEMBER 1989.
TRUE FAITH

AHUH-
HHEM.
DEAR
LORD...

19TH SEPTEMBER 1989.
PISS OFF!
BLOODY HELL, NIGE! WE ONLY ASKED—
YEAH, ONLY ABOUT FIFTY TIMES. I'M NOT COMING DOWN THE ARCADES, ALRIGHT?
151 A

YEAH, BUT WE KEEP ASKIN' 'CAUSE WE WANNA KNOW WHY, NIGE.
BUT I DON'T HAVE TO TELL YOU, KEVIN—
GIT

SODDIN' OBVIOUS, INNIT? NIGE'S AFTER THAT BIBLE THUMPER WIV THE KNOCKERS... YOU KNOW, WOSSERNAME... ANGELA.
HE'S OFF TO THE BLOODY SCRIPTURE UNION MEETING.
GIT

LISTEN, PERVERT—
ANGELA HYMAN? YOU TIT, NIGE! GOLDEN GIRL ISN'T INTERESTED IN YOU!
GIT

I SAID I DON'T HAVE TO TELL YOU WHAT I'M—
OH, SCREW YOU. WE'LL LEAVE YOU TO YOUR BIBLE STUDY...

WANKERS...

OH.
MR. HUNT.
SIR.

DON'T "OH MR. HUNT SIR" ME, GIBSON. I JUST HEARD YOU SWEARING IN SCHOOL.
SORRY.

SORRY WHAT?!
S-SORRY, SIR.

YOU REALLY ARE PATHETIC, GIBSON.

YOU NEVER DO ANYTHING WORTHWHILE. I NEVER SEE YOU ON THE RUGBY PITCHES. YOU DON'T DRESS PROPERLY... YOU'VE GOT NO RESPECT FOR YOURSELF!
GOT NO RESPECT FOR YOU, YOU OLD TURD...

YOU'RE A WASTE OF TIME, GIBSON. YOU'RE USELESS.
FIFTY LINES ON MY DESK BY TOMORROW. RULE SIX—THE ONE ABOUT SWEARING.
YES, SIR.

YOU SHOULD GO TO THE SCRIPTURE UNION MEETING, GIBSON. MIGHT LEARN A BIT OF RESPECT FOR YOURSELF. AND FOR OTHER PEOPLE.
THAT'S IMPORTANT, TOO, YOU KNOW.
YOU'RE ONLY GOING SO YOU CAN EYE UP THE GOD-FEARING TALENT, YOU OLD GIT. THEN YOU'LL LAUGH ABOUT IT LATER WITH THAT PACK OF MISSING LINKS YOU CALL A RUGBY TEAM.

WHO AM I TRYING TO KID? THAT'S THE REASON I'M GOING.
NO IT ISN'T.
OKAY, IT IS. BUT I WON'T LAUGH ABOUT IT LATER WITH MY MATES.

12TH SEPTEMBER 1989.
...AND THANK YOU, LORD, FOR, UM, MY NEW JOB.
FOR MAKING ME "TERRY ADAIR, TOILET CLEANER PRODUCTS' SALESMAN."

UM...

UM...OH YES! MY NEW JOB WHICH WILL PROVIDE A GOOD HOME FOR MY FAMILY. IT IS THEM...ER, THEY WHOM I WANT TO TALK TO YOU ABOUT TODAY, UM, LORD.

AS YOU KNOW, LORD... WELL, YOU WOULD... MY WIFE IS IN THE THRONGS...ER, PANGS OF CHILDBIRTH AS WE SPEAK. I HAVE COME TO ASK...ER BEG YOU FOR THEIR SAFE DELIVERANCE THROUGH THE ORDEAL.

I KNOW THAT...UM...NOT TO SEEM PRESUMPTUOUS OR ANYTHING, LORD...THAT I NEED ONLY ASK AND YOU WILL WATCH OVER THEM BOTH.
UH... ASK AND IT SHALL BE GIVEN UNTO YOU, AS IT SAYS. UM... THE BIBLE, I MEAN.

PLEASE KEEP THEM SAFE, LORD. I LOVE THEM MORE THAN ANYTHING.

ER... EXCEPT FOR YOU, LORD.

19TH SEPTEMBER 1989.
WHAT A LOAD OF CRAP.
SO, WITH OUR OPENING PRAYER CONCLUDED, WE'LL GO ONTO THE READINGS.
EXIT

BLOODY ZOMBIES SPOUTING CRAP AND TRYING TO BRAIN-WASH ME. AND HERE I AM, JUST TO GET A GLIMPSE OF ANGELA HYMAN.
AND HERE'S THE FIRST SPEAKER...
I MEAN, WHAT AM I?

...ANGELA HYMAN.
A CHAUVINIST... OR SOMETHING...

THANK YOU, RICHARD.
YOU KNOW, A LOT OF PEOPLE ASK ME ABOUT GOD...

AND IT CAN BE A BIT CONFUSING. BUT YOU ARE ALL YOUNG AND CAN START TO LEARN GOD'S LESSONS EARLY...
OH GOD... OH CHRIST... OH JESUS...

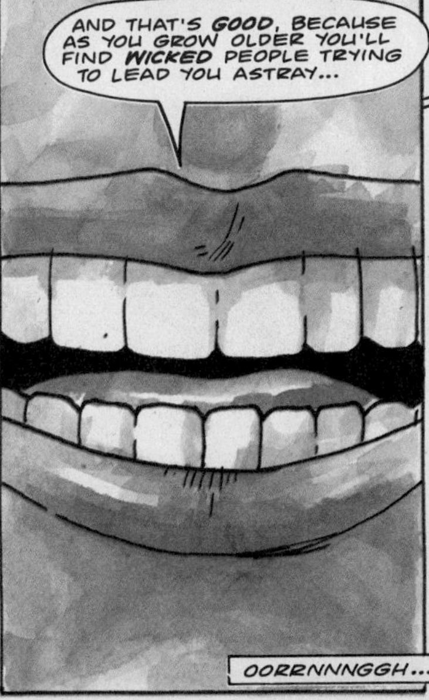
AND THAT'S GOOD, BECAUSE AS YOU GROW OLDER YOU'LL FIND WICKED PEOPLE TRYING TO LEAD YOU ASTRAY...
OORRNNNGGH...

PEOPLE WITH THEIR OWN PLANS FOR THE SERVANTS OF THE LORD.

12TH SEPTEMBER 1989.

MR. ADAIR? MR. TERENCE ADAIR?
YES?

COULD I HAVE A WORD, MR. ADAIR? THROUGH HERE, PLEASE.

IS IT MY WIFE, DOCTOR? IS SHE ASKING FOR ME?
UH... NOT EXACTLY, MR. ADAIR.
LOOK, I'D LIKE YOU TO PREPARE YOURSELF FOR A SHOCK...

I'M SORRY, MR. ADAIR, BUT YOUR WIFE DIED OF MASSIVE INTERNAL HAEMORRHAGING SIX MINUTES AGO. SHE GAVE BIRTH TO A MALE INFANT WHO... UH...
WELL, I'M AFRAID HE ONLY LIVED FOR A MINUTE. THERE WAS NOTHING WE COULD DO.

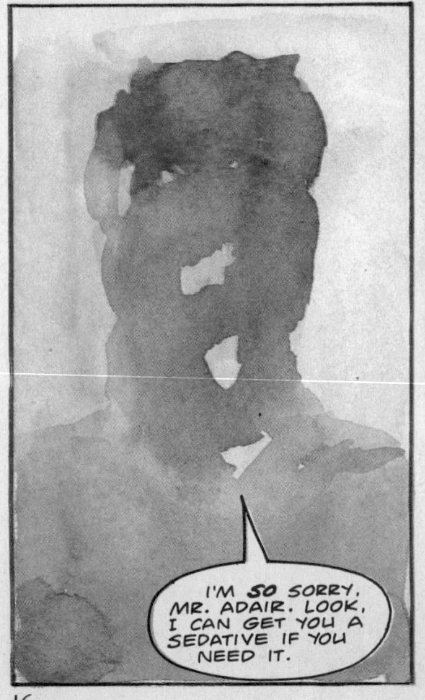
I'M SO SORRY, MR. ADAIR. LOOK, I CAN GET YOU A SEDATIVE IF YOU NEED IT.

MR. ADAIR?

19TH SEPTEMBER 1989.
UH, YEAH, I'M SURE IT DID TURN TO WINE BUT I JUST DON'T SEE HOW YOU CAN GO IN FOR ALL THE "WOMEN ARE WICKED" BITS —
BUT WE ALL HAVE TO KNOW OUR PLACES IN THE SIGHT OF GOD, NIGEL.

THAT'S JUST BLIND FAITH, ISN'T IT? I MEAN, IF A POLITICIAN TOLD YOU TO RELY ON THAT YOU'D TELL HIM TO F...ER, TO WISE UP.
BUT IT ISN'T A POLITICIAN, NIGEL. IT'S GOD.

UHHEHH...DON'T YOU EVER FEEL LIKE LETTING GO A LITTLE, THOUGH? IT MUST BE A BIT BORING, REPRESSING ALL THOSE URGES —
I HAVE TO. I CAN'T BE WEAK, NIGEL. IT'S A SIN.

I APPEAR TO BE GETTING NOWHERE FAST...
IN THAT CASE, I SUPPOSE YOU WOULDN'T, LIKE, WANT TO GO DOWN THE RED ROVER TONIGHT, HMMM?
WHY NOT?
61

UH...WELL, IT'S JUST THAT IT'S A PUB, YOU KNOW?
OH, THAT'S OKAY. I'M ALLOWED TO ENJOY MYSELF, NIGEL!
61
GREAT! I'LL —
I CAN HAVE AN ORANGE JUICE.

YEAH. YEAH, RIGHT! ORANGE JUICE. SEE YOU THERE ABOUT EIGHT, OKAY?
OKAY. BYEEE!
WELL, BUGGER ME. THIS IS GONNA BE BRILLIANT...

15TH SEPTEMBER 1989.
MAN THAT IS BORN OF WOMAN HATH BUT A SHORT TIME TO LIVE, AND IS FULL OF MISERY. HE COMETH UP, AND IS CUT DOWN, LIKE A FLOWER. HE FLEETH AS IT WERE A SHADOW...

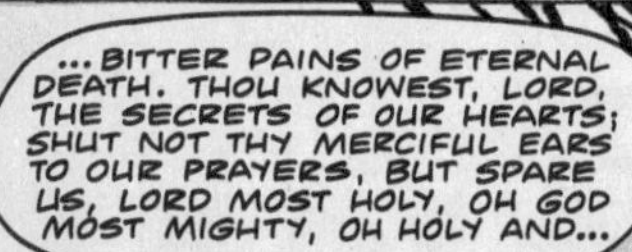
...BITTER PAINS OF ETERNAL DEATH. THOU KNOWEST, LORD, THE SECRETS OF OUR HEARTS; SHUT NOT THY MERCIFUL EARS TO OUR PRAYERS, BUT SPARE US, LORD MOST HOLY, OH GOD MOST MIGHTY, OH HOLY AND...

...UNTO HIMSELF THE SOULS OF OUR DEAR SISTER AND HER CHILD HERE DEPARTED. WE THEREFORE COMMIT THEIR BODIES TO THE GROUND:
EARTH TO EARTH, ASHES TO ASHES, DUST TO DUST.
AMEN.
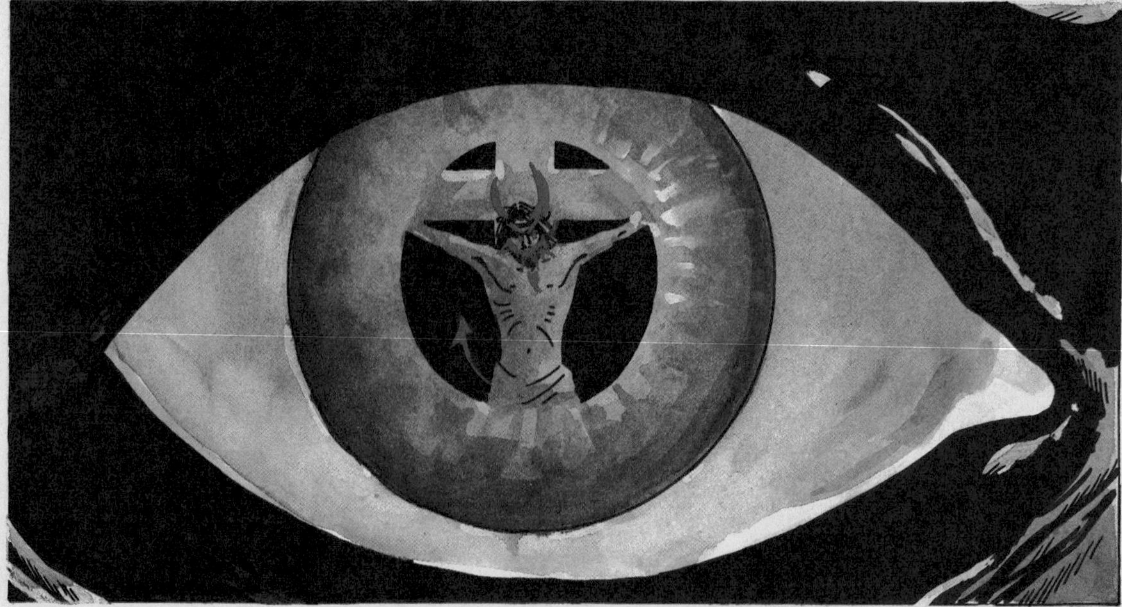

WHAT A BLOODY AWFUL THING TO HAPPEN TO HIM.
MMM, YES. POOR OLD GERRY.

APPARENTLY MOST OF THESE PEOPLE WERE LAURA'S FRIENDS. WELL, I AM, ANYWAY.
ME, TOO.
MMM... WELL, ANYWAY, IT'LL BE ROUGH ON GERRY GETTING OVER IT. NOT MANY TO TURN TO, YOU KNOW?
MMM.

STILL, I EXPECT HE'LL GET OVER IT.
MMMM.
HE'S YOUNG, AFTER ALL, AND TIME'S A GREAT HEALER.
MMM.

THANK YOU BOTH FOR COMING—
S...S'ARRIGHT, MATE. AN' LISSHEN, DON' WOORRY BOUDDIT, 'KAY? S'NOO PROBLEM. AFFER ALL, S'PLENTY MORE FISH INNA SHEA.
FOR CHRIST'S SAKE, DAVID! SHE DIDN'T LEAVE HIM— SHE BLOODY DIED!

DON'T WORRY ABOUT HIM, GERRY. HE'S HAD A FEW.
MMM. IT'LL BE ALRIGHT, GERRY.
MMM. JUST TAKE IT EASY FOR A WHILE, GERRY.

IT'S TERRY.
MY NAME'S TERRY.

MMMM.

ALL GONE

LAURA CAROL ADAIR
1967-1989
"RESTING WITH OTHER ANGELS"
SAMUEL PATRICK ADAIR
10·10-10·11am
12th SEPTEMBER 1989
"HIS CANDLE BLEW OUT EARLY"

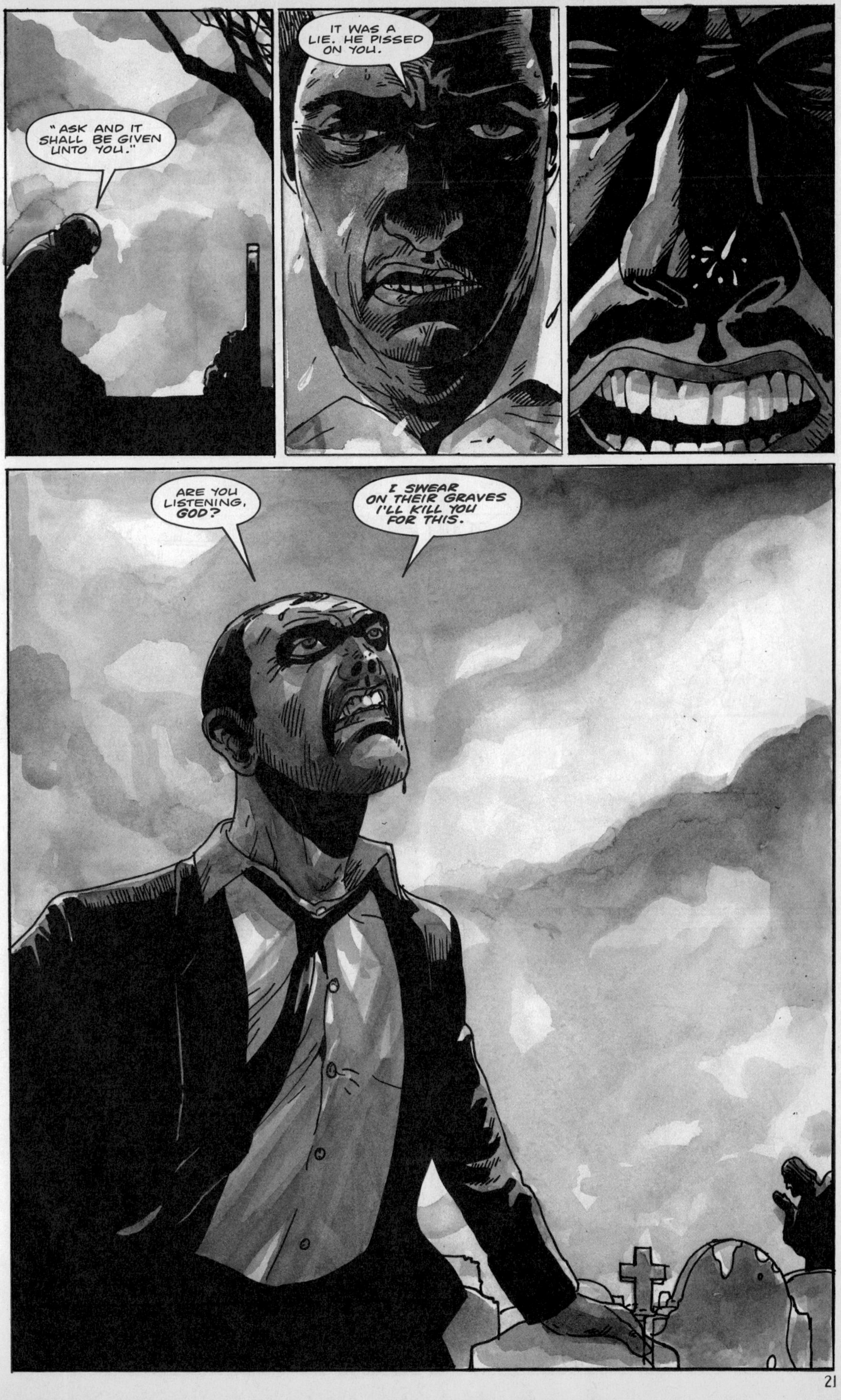

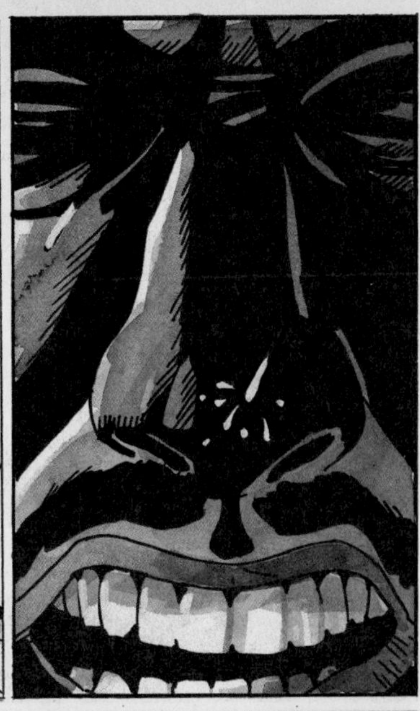

ARE YOU LISTENING, GOD?

I SWEAR ON THEIR GRAVES I'LL KILL YOU FOR THIS.

19TH SEPTEMBER 1989.
PIZZA REGURGIATO
HERE WE GO, HERE WE GO, HERE WE GO...

HERE WE ARE.

RIGHT, ANGELA. HERE'S WHERE YOU FALL TOTALLY UNDER MY SPELL.

I MEAN, UH, WHERE WE FORM A MEANINGFUL, EQUAL CARING RELATIONSHIP.
DON'T WANT TO BE A SEXIST ABOUT THIS...

NIGEL! OVER HERE!

OH, NO...

WE WERE DELIGHTED YOU WERE SO INTERESTED IN OUR MEETING, NIGEL.
YEAH, IT'S GREAT TO SEE PEOPLE COMING ALONG AND, Y'KNOW, GETTING INVOLVED, INSTEAD OF JUST IGNORING US.
UH...

ANYWAY, I TOLD MY FRIENDS YOU WANTED TO TALK SOME MORE ABOUT IT, AND HERE WE ARE!
THAT'S... THAT'S REALLY GREAT, THANKS.

I'LL JUST GET A DRINK THEN, YEAH?
SURE, NIGEL. THE COKE'S GOOD WITH ICE.
THANKS, MIKE. I'LL, UH, BEAR IT IN MIND.

PINT OF STELLA, MATE.
AAOOWWW... SHIT!
SHE THINKS I WANNA BE A BLOODY CHRISTIAN! SHE DOESN'T REALISE—
ALSO, SHE SEEMS TO BE WITH THAT BLOND GIT MIKE HENSON...

DON'T KNOW WHAT YOUR PROBLEM IS, MATE.
BUT YOU LOOK JUST THE WAY I FEEL.

# 2: The Wolf and the Sheep

AHHH... NEEDED THAT!
SO, WHAT'RE WE TALKING ABOUT?

WELL, WE ALL KNOW HOW DIFFICULT IT IS WHEN YOU'VE DECIDED TO BE A CHRISTIAN. I MEAN, WE'VE ALL BEEN THERE OURSELVES.
IN-DEED.
YOUR FRIENDS MAKE FUN OF YOU, FOR ONE THING. I HAD A TERRIBLE TIME WHEN I FIRST JOINED THE SCRIPTURE UNION.

YEAH, THAT'S REALLY GREAT, BUT I HAVEN'T ACTUALLY JOINED YET, YOU KNOW?
OH SURE... SURE...
SO YOU NEED HELP WITH YOUR DECISION, YEAH? WHAT EXACTLY D'YOU WANT TO KNOW?

JUST LITTLE THINGS, REALLY... HOW DO I FIND FAITH... WHAT BEING A CHRISTIAN MEANS IN TODAY' SOCIETY... WHICH PRAYERS DO I USE...
RIGHT, WELL, WE CAN—

AND, OF COURSE, WHY YOU THINK I WOULD WANT TO FOLLOW SUCH A MINDLESS COP-OUT PHILOSOPHY AS CHRISTIANITY ANYWAY.
YOU PRICKS.
PHWOOFFSST!!

NIGEL! WHAT D'YOU—
WHAT'S THE MATTER WITH YOU, GIBSON? WHY—
OOOH, IT'S "GIBSON" NOW, IS IT?

YES IT IS! WHAT D'YOU MEAN BY ALL THAT? WHAT'S SO MINDLESS ABOUT US?
WELL, NOT TO PUT TOO FINE A POINT ON IT, YOU'VE GOT NO MINDS OF YOUR OWN. YOU GO AROUND PREACHING FROM SOME BOOK COBBLED TOGETHER TWO THOUSAND YEARS AGO—

HOW DARE YOU!
HEY, YOU ASKED, GOLDEN BOY.
I THOUGHT YOU WERE INTERESTED...

UH, TAKE IT EASY, GUYS.
LOOK, NIGEL, WHAT'S YOUR PROBLEM WITH GOD?
HE DOESN'T EXIST, FOR STARTERS. BUT THEN THAT'S MORE SORT OF HIS PROBLEM, ISN'T IT?
OH YES, THAT'S RIGHT— JUST MAKE FUN. THAT'S ALL YOUR SORT CAN DO, ISN'T IT?

"MY"
"SORT."
WHAT SORT'S THAT, MIKE?

YOU NEVER ACHIEVE ANYTHING! YOU'VE GOT NOTHING OF YOUR OWN AND ALL YOU CAN DO IS MAKE FUN OF PEOPLE WHO HAVE —
YEAH?
SO WHAT DO YOU HAVE THAT'S SO GREAT?

I'M A LOT BETTER OFF THAN YOU, GIBSON! I'M ON THE RUGBY TEAM, I'M DOING WELL AT MY "A" LEVELS, I'M COMPLETING MY DUKE OF EDINBURGH AWARD—
UH-HUH...
AND GOD IS WITH ME, GIBSON!

CHRIST, ARE YOU FULL OF SHIT OR WHAT?
EH?

YOU ARROGANT BASTARD. D'YOU THINK I'D WANT ANY OF THAT CRAP? YOU THINK THAT'S WHAT I WANT TO ACHIEVE?
HEY, I THINK MOST PEOPLE WOULD AGREE I'D DONE PRETTY WELL—
PISS OFF! JUST BECAUSE YOU WANT IT, EVERYONE ELSE HAS TO WANT IT, YEAH?
BECAUSE YOU'RE BLOODY GOLDEN BOY.

THAT'S THE TROUBLE WITH YOUR SORT, HENSON, AND THERE'S PLENTY LIKE YOU. YOU THINK EVERYONE HAS THE SAME AIMS AS YOU, THAT YOU'RE THE EXAMPLE TO FOLLOW.
WELL, THAT IS SO MUCH BULLSHIT. I'VE GOT MY OWN VALUES, THANKS.
OH, WHAT ARE YOU TALKING ABOUT?

I'M TALKING ABOUT DOING MY OWN THINKING. NOT HAVING IT HANDED TO ME ON A PLATE WITH SOME BLOODY VICAR AND HIS MIND CONTROL—
RUBBISH! I'M A CHRISTIAN AND I CAN THINK FOR MYSELF!

GOD LOOKS AFTER PEOPLE, GIBSON. ALL HE ASKS IS THAT THEY GIVE HIM THEIR LOVE—
AND THEIR FREE WILL.
NO, GIBSON. YOU'RE JUST SO TWISTED UP—

SHUT YOUR FACE.

WHO—
YOU'D BETTER WATCH OUT, SON. YOU'D JUST BETTER.
LOOK, I—

SHUT UP! I'VE BEEN LISTENING TO YOU GOING ON ABOUT GOD, ARSEHOLE. HE'S ON YOUR SIDE, IS HE? HE LOVE'S YOU?
YES, HE—
BOLLOCKS! HE DOESN'T GIVE A SHIT! YOU WAIT! YOU JUST WAIT UNTIL YOUR RISING MAIN STOP VALVE IS LOOSE!

BECAUSE THAT'S WHEN IT COUNTS, SON. THAT'S WHEN IT MATTERS. AND WHEN YOU'RE DISAPPEARING ROUND THE 'S' BEND AND GOD STILL HASN'T TURNED UP WITH A HALF-INCH WRENCH AND A PLUNGER...
WELL, THEN YOU'LL REALISE JUST HOW MUCH THE GOOD LORD CARES ABOUT YOU.
I KNOW. IT HAPPENED TO ME.

BUT DON'T WORRY, SON. DON'T CONCERN YOURSELF.
YOU SEE, GOD ISN'T GOING TO BE **AROUND** TO CRACK ANYBODY ELSE'S CISTERN...

BECAUSE I'M GOING TO **KILL** HIM.

ARE YOU ALRIGHT, MIKE?
Y-Y-YEAH. FINE. I'M FINE...
JUST SOME NUT, MIKE. DON'T WORRY.

NIGEL, WHERE ARE YOU GOING?
HMMM? OH, JUST WANTED TO CHECK THAT BLOKE OUT—
HE'S JUST SOME LOONEY.

WELL, HE **SEEMED** QUITE INTERESTING...
OH COME **ON**, NIGEL. MIKE'S HAD A SHOCK—

**BUGGER** MIKE, YOU DOZY BITCH!
CHRIST, ARE YOU STUPID OR SOMETHING? THE ONLY REASON I'M HERE IS I THOUGHT I HAD A CHANCE OF GETTING INTO YOUR **KNICKERS**.
I **DIDN'T** EXPECT YOU TO BRING **THESE** DICKS ALONG FOR A BLOODY **DISCUSSION GROUP!!**

WELL, THAT'S GOT ME DAMNED TO THE LOWEST PIT OF HELL FOR ALL ETERNITY.
WHAT TO DO FOR THE REST OF THE EVENING, I WONDER...

AHH, THERE'S THE NUTCASE. MAY AS WELL SEE WHAT HE'S UP TO.
SUN

THE KILLING GOD BIT SOUNDED LIKE A GOOD LAUGH. MAYBE HE'LL PUT THE HEAD ON A CHURCH OR SOMETHING.
AND WHAT WAS ALL THAT ABOUT CISTERNS AND VALVES, FOR GOD'S SAKE?
SHAZ

NOTHING LIKE A LUNATIC FOR A LITTLE AMUSEMENT... AND I CAN ALWAYS SPLIT IF HE THROWS A WOBBLY.

BESIDES, HE'S PROBABLY COMPLETELY HARMLESS.

# 3: The Scheme of Things

BOLLOCKS
HE' DY HEIGHTS

Yale
COULDN'T HURT...

I BET *THAT* COULD, THOUGH.
JESUS CHRIST.

DIARY
1989

AUGUST 21ST, 1989.
I hope I can afford the hire purchase payment on my new lawnmower this month...

SEPTEMBER 10TH, 1989.
Sold a big order to Mr. Neil Butler, a lab worker. The weather was quite changeable today. I wonder if it will snow this Christmas? It never seems to snow anymore.

SEPTEMBER 11TH, 1989.
Laura went into hospital today. I hope she is alright. I'm going to pop into church tomorrow on the way to the hospital. I'm sure God will help her. Just think! I am to be a father!

HMMM?
MON 11
TUES 12
WED 13
THUR 14
FRI 15
SAT 16
SUN 17

SEPTEMBER 19TH, 1989.
And so it goes.
The deed is done, the chain is pulled, the toilet flushes, the pan empties, the ball lowers.
My pan is empty. My ball is lowered.

And then things go awry. The pan should refill, the ball should rise again.
But mine has not, and so my pan is empty still, and my ball is lowered still. Woe is me.

God has failed me. God has become a blockage.
I need a plunger.

It is the nineteenth of September. I have begun my mission. I will rid myself of the blockage, and in so doing will save the world.
For God is the world's blockage too.

I will go out unto his houses and I will burn. And I will kill.

Tonight I go to the church in which God first betrayed me, the place where I sat like a fool and prayed.
And it is only the first.

I will keep burning and killing until God shows his face. And he will, because so many of his servants and houses will be destroyed.
He will want to meet his nemesis.

And then I will look into the face of God.
And with all the reverence due to a blockage in the "S"-bend of the world...

...I will unblock him.
I will snuff him out.

SHITSHITSHITSHITSHIT!

GET THE PIGS, GET THE PIGS, GET THE PIGS—

EASY DOES IT FOR GOD'S SAKE...

BLOCKAGE.
VERY BAD.

4: The Lawmaker
NOW LOOK, UH, HOW ABOUT LETTING ME GO? I MEAN, YOU'VE OBVIOUSLY GOT A BIT OF A PROBLEM HERE, BUT—
QUIET.
SIT DOWN AT THE TABLE. KEEP YOUR HANDS AWAY FROM WHAT'S ON IT.

O-OKAY. SURE.
SHUT YOUR MOUTH. SPEAK ONLY WHEN ANSWERING MY QUESTIONS.

NOW THEN... LET US SPEAK OF YOUR FUTURE.

OR, PERHAPS, LET US DECIDE IF YOU ARE TO HAVE ONE.

HMMM...

HAVEN'T WE ALREADY MET?

Y-Y-YES. AT THE, UM, THE PUB. THE RED ROVER. YOU HAD A GO AT THE PEOPLE I WAS WITH.
THAT'S RIGHT...

THE FOOL WHO THOUGHT GOD'S DIRECTABLE JET WOULD CLEAN UNDER HIS RIM.
BUT YOU WERE DIFFERENT, WEREN'T YOU? THEY WERE ARGUING WITH YOU.

I...WELL, I DON'T GET ON VERY WELL WITH THEM, YOU KNOW? THAT'S SORT OF WHY I FOLLOWED YOU. I LIKED ALL THE STUFF ABOUT KILLING GOD.
DID YOU NOW.

AND WHAT'S YOUR NAME, MY ATHEISTIC FRIEND?
NIGEL. NIGEL GIBSON. I GO TO SCHOOL WITH THE PRATS FROM THE PUB.

I DIDN'T ASK YOU WHERE YOU WENT TO SCHOOL, NIGEL. I ONLY ASKED YOUR NAME.
R-RIGHT, YEAH. SORRY.

AS YOU SAID EARLIER, I HAVE A PROBLEM.
YOU FOLLOWED ME FROM THE PUB, AND YOU ENTERED MY FLAT. YOU SAW MY GUNS AND BOMBS, AND I'M SURE YOU READ MY JOURNAL AS WELL.

WHATEVER WILL I DO WITH YOU?

I COULD GIVE YOU DEATH. YOU KNOW ABOUT MY MISSION. YOU'RE A THREAT.
BUT...

I SENSE A CERTAIN... KINSHIP WITH YOU, NIGEL. YOU HAVE A CERTAIN HATRED, OR AT LEAST REJECTION, OF MY ENEMY.
WHAT, LIKE, THE CHRISTIANS? OH, FOR SURE. BASTARDS, THE LOT OF THEM.
MM-HMMM.

YOU KNOW MY MISSION, NIGEL. I'M RIDDING THE WORLD OF THE BLOCKAGE, BEFORE THE WHOLE SPLIT-PIN GROMMET ASSEMBLY COMES LOOSE AND THERE'S AN OVERFLOW IN THE CISTERN.
BUT WHAT'LL WE DO WHEN THE BLOCKAGE IS GONE? WHEN THERE'S NO GOD ANYMORE?

WELL, I KNOW WHAT TO DO. I'M GOING TO BE MY OWN GOD.
SO I MIGHT AS WELL BE YOURS, TOO, EH?
UH... YEAH...

I WON'T GIVE YOU DEATH, NIGEL. OH NO. I'LL GIVE YOU LAW.

AND I SPAKE UNTO MYSELF, SAYING, THOU SHALT SAY TO NIGEL, WHOSOEVER HE BE OF THE CHILDREN OF MR. AND MRS. GIBSON, THAT GRASSETH MY HOLY MISSION UNTO THE POLICE, HE SHALL SURELY BE PUT TO DEATH!

FOR I WILL SET MY FACE AGAINST THAT MAN, AND WILL CUT HIM OFF FROM THE BLOOD SUPPLY TO HIS BRAIN, BECAUSE HE WILL SURELY HAVE FLUSHED ME DOWN THE PIPE!

SANCTIFY YOURSELF, THEREFORE, AND KEEP YOUR MOUTH SHUT, FOR I AM THE LORD YOUR PERSON WITH A SAWN-OFF TWELVE BORE STANDING VERY NEAR YOU!

AND YE SHALL KEEP MY STATUTES AND DO THEM: I AM THE LORD WHICH THREATENS YOUR CONTINUED EXISTENCE!
IS THAT CLEAR?
UM, YEAH. CRYSTAL.

ER...

WELL, THAT'S IT, NIGEL. YOU CAN GO NOW.
UH... RIGHT. GOODBYE, THEN.
'BYE.

BRAINDEAD FUC
LUNATIC BLOODY UNBELIEVABLE LUNATIC JESUS GOD IN HEAVEN ABOVE—

YOU ALRIGHT THERE, SON?
HE...HE DID IT...

HE DID IT! THIS! HE DID THIS!
CALM DOWN, SON. WHAT—
THE BLOKE WHO DID THIS! I KNOW HIM!

HE'S A BLOODY NUTCASE! HE'S TRYING TO KILL GOD, AND, AND—
SLOW DOWN, NOW. TAKE IT EASY.

OKAY, LOOK, THERE'S THIS GUY, RIGHT? AND HE THINKS THE WORLD IS KIND OF A TOILET, AND GOD IS STUCK IN IT, OKAY? AND HE DID THIS, LIKE THE CHURCH—

SO AS TO...UH... KILL GOD. THE, UM, BLOCKAGE...UM...
DID HE REALLY. WELL, I SUPPOSE IT'S THE SORT OF THING YOU'D DO IF YOU THOUGHT THE WORLD WAS A TOILET, HMM?

THIS ISN'T A LAUGHING MATTER—
KLANGG!
HERE! WOSSAT?

JUST STAY WHERE YOU ARE, OKAY? I WANNA WORD WITH YOU WHEN I'VE HAD A LOOK IN THE ALLEY.

HERE, WHAT'S— UCCHH!
AAARRCCCHHORRP!
UHHHH...

LAWBREAKER.

HE'S TRYING TO ESCAPE ME.
5: The Prodigal Son

HE WON'T, THOUGH. HE'LL RUN FOR A WHILE. THEN HE'LL REALISE HE'S NOT EVEN THINKING ABOUT WHERE HE'S GOING, SO HE'LL STOP AND THINK AND THEN HEAD FOR HOME.

AT HOME HE CAN BE WARM AND SECURE, AND HE CAN BLURT OUT THE AWFUL STORY ABOUT THE LUNATIC WHO SET FIRE TO A CHURCH AND THREATENED HIM WITH A SHOTGUN.
HE CAN CALM DOWN AND BREATHE EASILY AGAIN, WHILE GOOD OLD DAD PHONES THE POLICE TO GET IT ALL SORTED OUT.

31 ELMGROVE AVENUE, CLAPHAM.
THAT'S NOT TOO FAR.

...HOWEVER, MRS. THATCHER STATED TODAY IN THE COMMONS THAT SHE WAS SATISFIED THAT THE POLICE HAD ACTED WITH ADMIRABLE RESTRAINT.
MMM... ELEVEN O' CLOCK. NIGEL'S NOT BACK YET.
ELEVEN ISN'T SO LATE.

TO LABOUR CHEERS, MR. KINNOCK RESPONDED BY TELLING THE PRIME MINISTER TO F... EXCUSE ME, I'VE JUST BEEN HANDED SOME LATE NEWS.
HE'S GOT SCHOOL IN THE MORNING, THOUGH. OUGHT TO BE GETTING AN EARLY NIGHT.
THAT'S FAIR ENOUGH. I'LL HAVE A WORD WITH HIM WHEN HE GETS IN.

REPORTS ARE COMING IN OF AN ARSON ATTACK ON A CHURCH IN LONDON, NEAR CLAPHAM COMMON.
WOULD YOU, LOVE? I'D FEEL **SO** MUCH BETTER, WHAT WITH HIS 'A' LEVELS AND SO ON.

IT'S TOO EARLY TO DETERMINE THE DAMAGE, BUT ONE REPORT SUGGESTS THE LOCAL VICAR HAS BEEN HURT IN THE ATTACK.
I'LL TAKE CARE OF IT, DEAR. HE'S A GOOD LAD, IS NIGEL. A BIT QUIET, MAYBE, BUT HE'S A GOOD LAD.

HIS EXACT CONDITION IS UNKNOWN, HOWEVER.
HE'S A **PRAT**, DAD. ALL THE GIRLS THINK HE'S A **WEIRDO**. IT'S EMBARRASSING FOR ME, SOMETIMES.

WE NOW GO OVER LIVE TO BBC REPORTER JOHN POTTER, WHO HAS REACHED THE CHURCH WITH A CAMERA TEAM.
JOHN?
DON'T SAY THAT ABOUT YOUR BROTHER NOW, RUTH.

HUH, HUH, HUH... HOLY SHIT!

TAKE IT EASY, NOW. CALM DOWN. JUST CALM DOWN.

I'M GOING HOME. I'M GOING TO GO HOME WHERE I'LL BE SAFE AND I'LL CALL THE POLICE FROM THERE AND I DON'T CARE IF ANYONE HEARS ME TALKING TO MYSELF AND THINKS I'M MAD.
IF I DON'T HEAR A HUMAN VOICE I'LL BLOODY GO MAD.

ELMGROVE AVENUE

JESUS! JESUS CHRIST!

COME ON THEN, ARSEHOLE! COME AND TRY IT! COME ON!

LET'S SEE YOU DEAL WITH REX, YOU SON OF A BITCH! LET'S SEE YOU UNBLOCK A HUNDRED AND FIFTY POUND ALSATIAN.
27

HE'LL TEAR YOUR THROAT OUT, YOU BASTARD! HE'LL SAVE ME!
MY DOG—
29
MY SAVIOUR—

31

IT AMAZES ME THAT PEOPLE STILL THINK GOD IS THERE TO HELP THEM.
THIS BOY IS A FOOL... AND YET IS, PERHAPS, A BRAND THAT SHOULD BE PLUCKED FROM THE BURNING.

GOD HAS LET HIM DOWN. HIS FOUR FOOTED ANGEL OF DELIVERANCE HAS FALLEN TOO FAR TO DO ANY GOOD.
YOU JUST CAN'T RELY ON ANYONE THESE DAYS.

AAAOOW!?!

SO MUCH FOR YOUR SAVIOUR. FEET OF CLAY, WOULDN'T YOU AGREE?

YOU CAN... YOU CAN FIND ME ANY TIME YOU WANT, CAN'T YOU? AND YOU CAN KILL ANYONE WHO TRIES TO HELP ME.
I MIGHT AS WELL JUST GIVE UP.

NO, DON'T GIVE UP.

FOR THIS MY SON WAS DEAD, AND IS ALIVE AGAIN; HE WAS LOST, AND IS FOUND.
WE SHOULD MAKE MERRY, AND BE GLAD.

IT IS THY HAND THAT WILL JOIN WITH MINE IN FREEING THE RISING MAIN STOP VALVE AND LETTING THE CLEANSING WATERS ONCE MORE RUN FREE.
THOU ART EVER WITH ME IN MY MISSION...

...MY SON.

# 6: Godslayer

I HAD A NORMAL LIFE ONCE.

I WENT TO SCHOOL. I DID QUITE WELL, TOO. I HAD MY FRIENDS AND I WATCHED MOVIES AND LISTENED TO MUSIC AND READ THE N.M.E.
YOU KNOW.
THE WAY YOU DO.

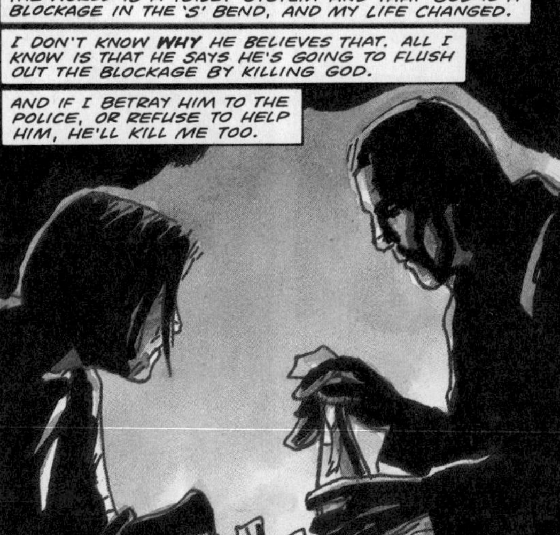
THEN ONE NIGHT I MET TERRY ADAIR, WHO BELIEVES THE WORLD IS A TOILET SYSTEM AND THAT GOD IS A BLOCKAGE IN THE 'S' BEND, AND MY LIFE CHANGED.
I DON'T KNOW WHY HE BELIEVES THAT. ALL I KNOW IS THAT HE SAYS HE'S GOING TO FLUSH OUT THE BLOCKAGE BY KILLING GOD.
AND IF I BETRAY HIM TO THE POLICE, OR REFUSE TO HELP HIM, HE'LL KILL ME TOO.

HE CONVINCED ME OF THAT LAST FACT BEYOND ANY SHADOW OF A DOUBT.
I BELIEVE HIM. I HAVE FAITH IN HIM.

GREAT FAITH.

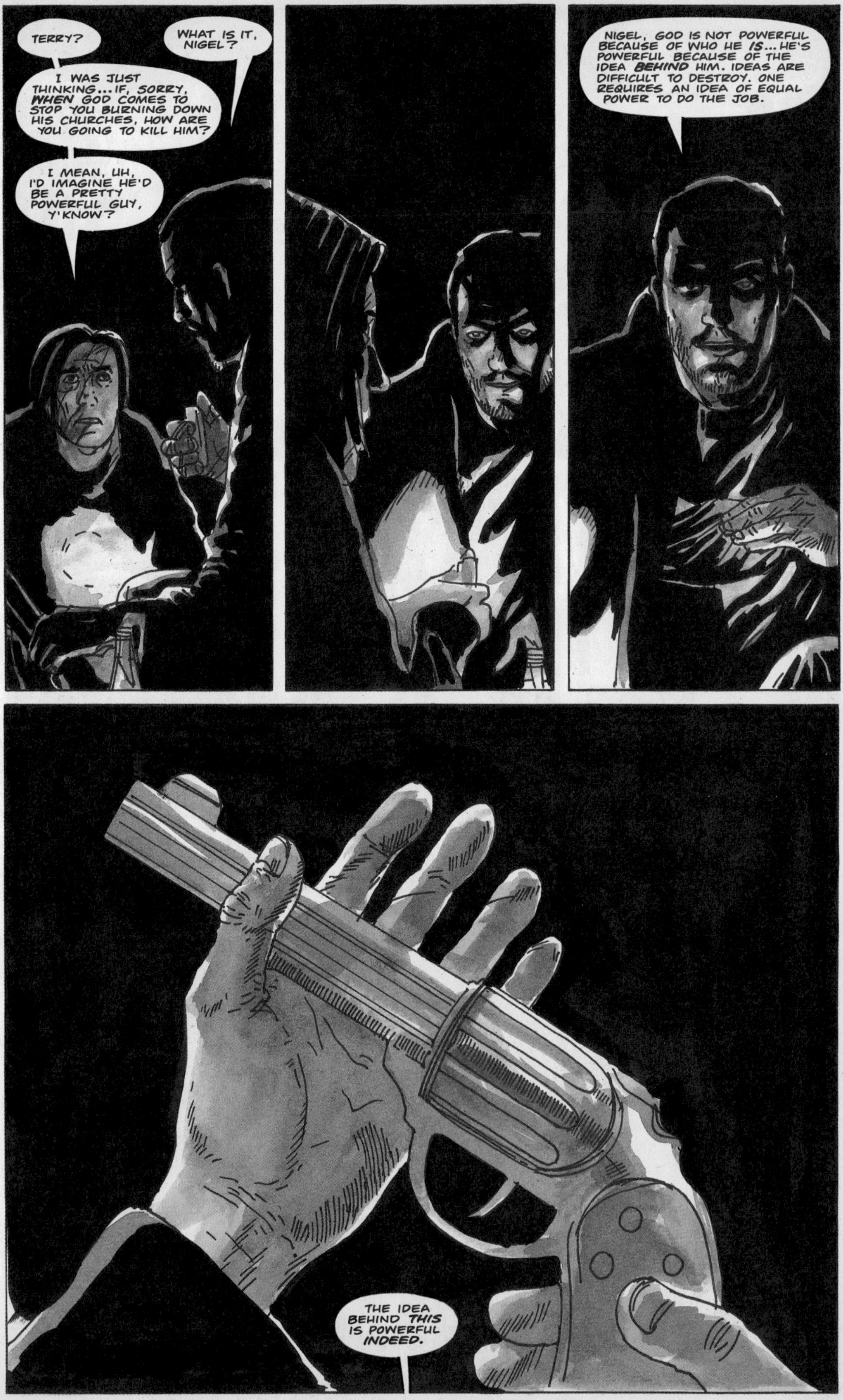

THE IDEA BEHIND ***THIS*** IS POWERFUL ***INDEED.***

THAT? TERRY, THAT'S JUST A GUN. A BIG GUN, BUT STILL JUST A GUN. WHAT'S SO GREAT ABOUT THE IDEA OF THAT?
IT HAS A MYTHOLOGY, NIGEL. IT HAS WORDS OF POWER.
EH?

"I KNOW WHAT YOU'RE THINKING, PUNK. YOU'RE THINKING, DID HE FIRE SIX SHOTS... OR ONLY FIVE?
"BUT BEIN' AS THIS IS A FORTY-FOUR MAGNUM, THE MOST POWERFUL HAND GUN IN THE WORLD, AND COULD BLOW YOUR HEAD RIGHT OFF, YOU'VE GOTTA ASK YOURSELF A QUESTION — DO I FEEL LUCKY?"

"WELL DO YA... PUNK?"

YOU SEE? PEOPLE KNOW THESE WORDS, NIGEL. THEY HAVE GREAT MEANING... THEY ARE EQUAL IN THE MINDS OF THE PEOPLE TO THE WORDS OF GOD.
THEY ARE MY WEAPONS TO DESTROY HIM.

MAYBE THE BASTARD WILL SHOW UP TONIGHT AND I'LL SHOW YOU WHAT I MEAN.

...GOT LUCKY. IT'S THE METHODIST ONE IN THE STOCKWELL ROAD.
NO SIR, NOT YET, NO POLICE. THE FIRE HASN'T REALLY TAKEN PROPERLY.
TWO MINUTES? RIGHT, SIR.

WHAT ON EARTH IS GOING ON HERE?! YOU MEN! STOP!

AAAOOOW... UH...UH... P-PLEASE...

YOU SERVE THE BLOCKAGE, DON'T YOU? WHERE IS HE?
AAAOOW... OH GOD—

WHERE IS HE?
AAAH! PLEASE, DON'T HURT ME, PLEASE—
WHERE?!

OW! PLEASE, I DON'T KNOW WHO YOU WANT! MY-MY LEG HURTS, PLEASE LET ME GO!
I NEED TO FIND THE BLOCKAGE! WHERE'S HE HIDING?!

EH?

THE BLOCKAGE STOPS THINGS FROM FLOWING AND MAKES IT ALL STAGNANT! LOOK, HERE. LOOK AT THIS! SEE? I CAN ONLY GET MY HAND IN A FEW INCHES! IT'S BLOCKED!
I...UHHH... I NEED A DOCTOR...

LOOK! IT'S BLOCKED!

GOD'S BLOCKED IT UP, DAMMIT!

BLOCKED! BLOCKED! BLOCKED!

UH...
YOU... YOU KILLED HIM...

NO, NO, NO. THE BLOCKAGE KILLED HIM. IF THE BLOCKAGE HADN'T BEEN THERE HE WOULD ONLY HAVE GOT HIS HEAD WET, YOU SEE?
THE BLOCKAGE MESSES EVERYONE UP.

SO DO YOU UNDERSTAND NOW, NIGEL?
WE'VE GOTTA GET OUT OF HERE NOW. THE POLICE —
YES, YES. BUT DO YOU UNDERSTAND?

IT'S-OOUF!

EEEARH! NO —
BASTARDS! YOU FRIGGING SONS OF — AUF!

COME ON! THE POLICE'LL BE HERE ANY SECOND!

GET OFF ME, DAMMIT!! BASTARDS! PIGS! SHITS!
KEEP THEM QUIET BACK THERE, WILL YOU?! ONLY ANOTHER MINUTE!

WELCOME TO MY HOME, GENTLEMEN.
HUH?

WHO THE HELL ARE YOU?
MY DEAR FELLOW, THERE'S NO NEED TO BE SO HOSTILE.
AFTER ALL, IF YOU PEOPLE HAVE SUCH A PENCHANT FOR BURNING DOWN CHURCHES...

...THEN I THINK WE'RE GOING TO BE VERY GOOD FRIENDS INDEED.

WHAT TERRY ADAIR DOES IS ILLOGICAL. IT'S INSANE. IT'S STUPID. IT CAUSES THE DEATHS OF INNOCENTS AND THE DESTRUCTION OF ALL THEY HOLD DEAR.
AND ALL OF THAT MEANS NOTHING TO HIM WHATSOEVER.
7: The Lord
I THINK TERRY ADAIR IS THE NEAREST I'LL EVER GET TO MEETING A GOD.

BUT IF TERRY ADAIR IS GOD...

WHO'S HE?

YOU ARE TERENCE ADAIR... AND CRINGING AT YOUR SIDE IS NIGEL GIBSON, CORRECT?
WHO ARE YOU?
IN A MOMENT, TERRY. NOW, CORRECT?

CORRECT.

IN-DEED.
ALWAYS GOOD TO ESTABLISH A PRECEDENT.

MY NAME, TO ANSWER YOUR QUESTION, IS CORNELIUS GARTEN.

THESE ARE MY TRUTH COMMANDOS.

WE'VE DECIDED THAT THE SOURCE OF THE WORLD'S SORROWS MUST BE REMOVED.

WE'RE GOING TO KILL GOD.

WE'VE BEEN OPERATING FOR SOME TIME NOW. ABOUT FIVE YEARS, I THINK. USING VARIOUS METHODS.

AT FIRST WE THOUGHT THAT PROMOTING *INCREDULITY* WOULD BE BEST.
WITH THE AID OF AN INSIDE MAN, WE INTRODUCED *LYSERGIC ACID DIETHYLAMIDE* TO THE CHIEF CONSTABLE OF A POLICE FORCE IN THE NORTH OF ENGLAND.
IN HIS COFFEE, NIGEL. IN HIS *COFFEE*.

*THAT* DIDN'T WORK.

SO WE TRIED TO PROVOKE A LITTLE *DISAFFECTION*.
A FOREIGN OFFICE CONTACT TIPPED OFF A PARAMILITARY GROUP IN THE LEBANON THAT AN ENVOY WAS BEING SENT BY THE CHURCH OF ENGLAND TO NEGOTIATE FOR HOSTAGES.

WELL, GOD HAD OBVIOUSLY GIVEN UP ON THE ENVOY, BUT NOBODY GAVE UP ON GOD.

SO WE DECIDED *DIRECT ACTION* WOULD BE BETTER. BURN CHURCHES AND SHOOT VICARS UNTIL GOD WAS DRAWN OUT OF HIDING, AND THEN KILL HIM.

FOUR NIGHTS AGO WE WERE PREPARING TO HIT THE ANGLICAN CHURCH AT CLAPHAM COMMON WHEN WE SAW THE VERY OPERATION *WE* HAD PLANNED BEING CARRIED OUT BEFORE OUR *EYES*.
BY *YOU*, TERRY.

QUITE A LITTLE ARSENAL, WOULDN'T YOU SAY?

WHAT DO YOU WANT?

RECRUITS.

WHY? WHY DO YOU WANT TO KILL GOD?
WHY? YOU ASK ME THAT?
MMM... GOOD POINT...

THE WORLD IS IN AGONY, TERRY. IT'S SPITTING BLOOD AND TEARING AT ITS GUTS AND HOWLING FOR RELIEF, BUT YOU DON'T YELL AT A CANCER.
YOU CUT IT OUT.

WILL YOU HELP ME CUT OUT THE CANCER, TERRY?

I'LL...I'LL HELP. BUT GOD'S NOT A CANCER. GOD'S A BLOCKAGE.
CANCER.
BLOCKAGE.
CANCER.
IT'S...UH... CANCER.
IT'S CANCER.
GOOD.
NOW, LET'S SEE WHAT WE'VE GOT IN THE WAY OF SCALPELS, EH?

IT'S FIVE THIRTY-TWO. NOBODY'S UP YET.
LET'S DO IT.

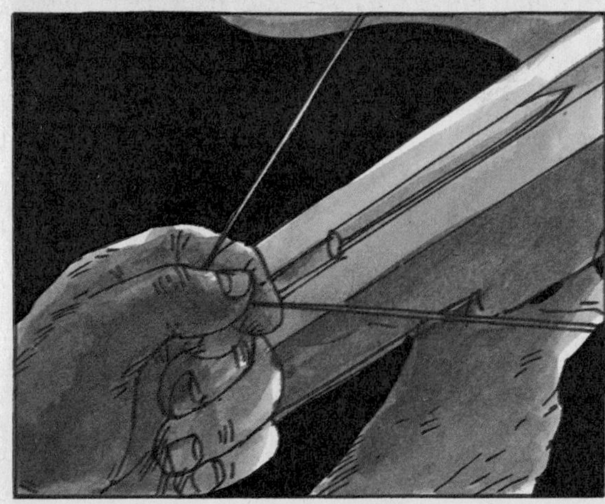

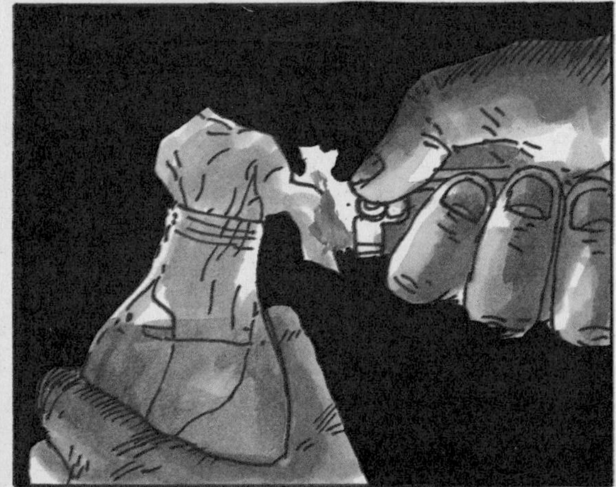

GOOD.

VERY GOOD.

I'M IMPRESSED. YOU HAVEN'T BEEN IN THE ORGANISATION **TWO HOURS** AND YOU'VE **ALREADY** PROVEN YOUR WORTH.
WELL **DONE.**

THANK YOU, CORNELIUS...

I THOUGHT TERRY ADAIR WAS A GOD. HE THREW OFF HIS RELIGION AND HE THOUGHT FOR HIMSELF AND, EVEN THOUGH HE WAS OFF HIS BLOODY **ROCKER**, HE WASN'T BEING LED ALONG LIKE A **SHEEP** ANYMORE.

BUT WITH THAT BASTARD CORNELIUS... WELL, TERRY'S BACK IN THE **FLOCK**.

WHICH MEANS **I'M** EVEN FURTHER UP **SHIT CREEK**.

## 8: The Fall

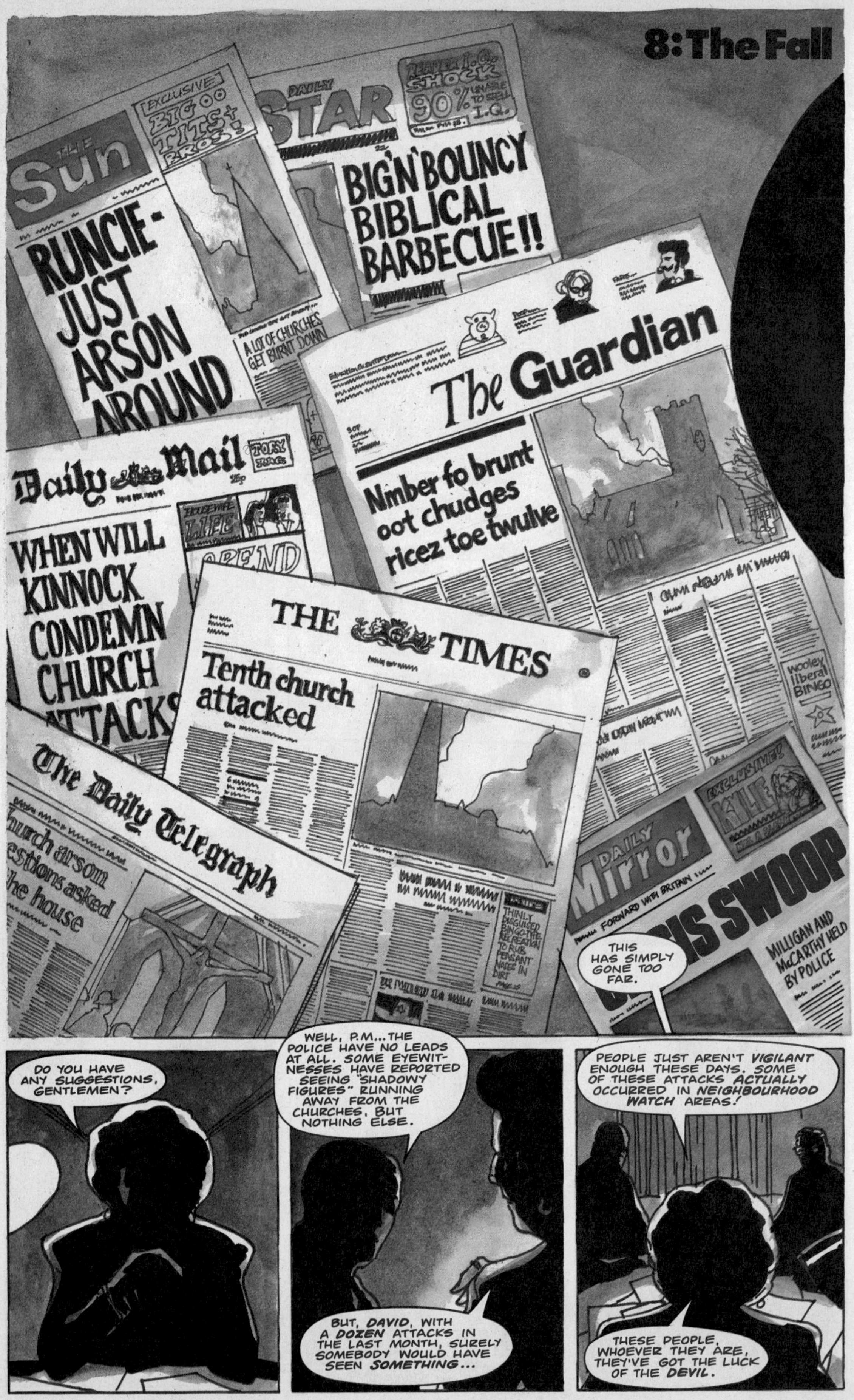

The Sun
EXCLUSIVE BIG 00 TITS + BROS!
RUNCIE - JUST ARSON AROUND
A LOT OF CHURCHES GET BURNT DOWN

DAILY STAR
READERS I.Q. SHOCK 90% UNABLE TO SPELL I.Q.
BIG 'N' BOUNCY BIBLICAL BARBECUE!!

The Guardian
Nmber fo brunt oot chudges ricez toe twulve
wooley liberal BINGO

Daily Mail
WHEN WILL KINNOCK CONDEMN CHURCH ATTACKS

THE TIMES
Tenth church attacked
THINLY DISGUISED BINGO THE RECREATION TO RUB PEASANT NOSES IN DIRT

The Daily Telegraph
Church arson questions asked in the house

DAILY Mirror
FORWARD WITH BRITAIN
EXCLUSIVE!
CRISIS SWOOP
MILLIGAN AND McCARTHY HELD BY POLICE

THIS HAS SIMPLY GONE TOO FAR.

P.M! I'VE HAD AN IDEA, P.M!
WHAT IS IT, TOM?

WELL — THE LUCK OF THE DEVIL! PERHAPS THAT'S IT! PERHAPS THEY'RE SATANISTS!
NO, TOM. I THOUGHT OF THAT MYSELF.

I WAS TALKING TO NORMAN LAST NIGHT — ONE OF OUR LITTLE CHATS, YOU KNOW — AND I ASKED HIM ABOUT IT. HE SAID IT ISN'T THE SATANISTS.
CERTAINLY NOT FROM *HIS* COVEN, ANYWAY.

WELL, P.M, PERHAPS IF WE CAN WORK OUT *WHY* THEY'RE DOING IT, WE CAN PREPARE BETTER FOR THE NEXT ATTACK.
*NO, DAVID.* NO, NO, *NO.*

*HOW* MANY TIMES DO I HAVE TO TELL YOU? I'M NOT INTERESTED IN *WHY* PEOPLE DO THINGS. I'M ONLY INTERESTED IN *STOPPING* THEM.

IT'S TIME TO TAKE *ACTION.*

BEING CONSCIOUS IS AN UTTER WANK THESE DAYS.
SUBURBAN TERRORIST BY NIGHT, PATHETIC SCHOOLGIT BY DAY.

MIND YOU, BEING UNCONSCIOUS ISN'T EXACTLY A LAUGH. LAST NIGHT I DREAMT I WAS DROWNING IN DOMESTOS WHILE TERRY ADAIR SHOVED A TOILET BRUSH UP HIS ARSE AND SANG "SILENT NIGHT."

MORNING, NIGEL.
MM.
OUT QUITE LATE THESE NIGHTS, AREN'T YOU, SON?

YEAH, WELL. NOW AND THEN.
YOU'RE LOOKING AWFULLY RUN DOWN, NIGEL. CAN'T BE GOOD FOR YOU.

YOU JUST DON'T SEEM YOURSELF THESE DAYS.
MMM... PROBABLY JUST A PHASE.

HE'S BEEN IN A "PHASE" ALL HIS LIFE, DAD. HE'S A REAL DIPPO.
NOW, NOW, RUTH. DON'T BE NASTY.

BY THE WAY... HAS ANYONE SEEN REX?
OH, YOU KNOW DOGS, DEAR. PROBABLY OFF WANDERING AROUND SOMEWHERE.

REX ISN'T WANDERING OFF ANYWHERE. REX IS AT THE BOTTOM OF THE THAMES WITH A BREEZEBLOCK TIED TO HIS TAIL.
AFTER ALL, IT WOULD'VE LOOKED PRETTY BAD IF MUM WOKE UP AND SAW THE BLOODY ANIMAL CRUCIFIED ON THE GARDEN GATE.

HERE WE GO AGAIN, THEN. OFF TO SCHOOL LIKE GOOD LITTLE CHILDREN.

ALRIGHT, NIGE!
'MORNING, JACKO.
'ERE, NIGE—HOW'S THE LOVE LIFE? BEEN A MONTH SINCE THE SCRIPTURE UNION THING, AN' IT LOOKS LIKE ANGELA'S STILL GOIN' WIV HENSON!

YEAH, I THOUGHT YOU WAS GONNA SWEEP HER OFF HER FEET, NIGE! WHAT HAPPENED?
NAH, KEV, DON'T YOU WORRY. OL' NIGE IS PROBABLY SHAGGIN' HER ON THE SLY, Y'KNOW?
THAT IT, NIGE? LITTLE AFFAIR BEHIND HENSON'S BACK, EH?

PROBABLY BEHIND ANGELA'S BACK KNOWIN' NIGE!!

BREATHE DEEP. COUNT TO A HUNDRED. KEEP CALM.
IT'S ONLY THE SIXTY-THIRD TIME HE'S MADE THAT JOKE, AFTER ALL.
THAT ISN'T SO BAD.

WELL, WELL, WELL.

LOOKS LIKE WE'RE ALL ALONE, GIBSON. JUST YOU AND ME.

DON'T FORGET GOD, MIKE. HE'S ALWAYS WITH US, ISN'T HE?

I HATE YOU, GIBSON!! YOU AND ALL THE SCUM OUT THERE LIKE YOU!!
AFTER WHAT YOU SAID TO ANGELA THAT NIGHT I OUGHT TO KILL YOU!

YOU'RE ONE HELL OF AN ADVERT FOR GOD'S LOVE, MIKE.

AAOW, CHRIST! THAT REALLY FRIGGIN' HURT, YOU BASTARD!!
DO BE QUIET NIGEL. JUST LIE THERE AT MY FEET WHERE YOU AND YOUR PATHETIC, MEANINGLESS EXIST-ENCE BELONG.

WHERE YOU ALWAYS WILL BELONG.

BALLS

YOU COULD FIND YOURSELF FACING ASSAULT CHARGES, GIBSON. YOU CAN'T JUST BRAIN SOMEONE WITH A CRICKET BAT AND EXPECT TO GET OFF WITH IT.
OH NO YOU CAN'T.

WHAT ON EARTH WERE YOU THINKING OF, GIBSON? YOU COULD HAVE FRACTURED HIS SKULL!
OH YES YOU COULD.

WELL, I HAD TO DEFEND MYSELF, SIR. I SHOWED HENSON SOMETHING HE DIDN'T LIKE VERY MUCH AND HE WENT A BIT WEIRD.
WHAT? WHAT DID YOU SHOW HIM?

HIMSELF.

WHAT THE HELL ARE YOU BABBLING ABOUT, BOY? MICHAEL HENSON IS ONE OF THIS SCHOOL'S FINEST PUPILS!
HE'S ABSOLUTELY VITAL TO THE RUGBY TEAM AND HE'S TOP OF MOST OF HIS CLASSES! AND HE'S A COMMITTED CHRISTIAN!
OH YES HE IS.

AND HERE YOU ARE, YOU LITTLE REPTILE, HAVING NEARLY KILLED HIM! AND YOU SO... SO...
WORTHLESS?

I GOT SUSPENDED FROM SCHOOL FOR A FORTNIGHT, DAD.
TCH. THAT'S NOT REALLY GOOD ENOUGH, NIGEL. GOING TO HAVE TO BUCK UP A BIT.
MMM. TRY HARDER, DEAR, PLEASE.
MORE GRAVY?

WELL, SHE WAS IN A REAL TEMPER TODAY.
YES... I WONDER WHAT THAT BUSINESS ABOUT TAKING ACTION MEANT?
GENTS-CABINET OFFICE

CONFERENCE ROOM-CABINET
PROBABLY THE USUAL OVER REACTION.
PROBABLY, YES... OH, HOW ANNOYING! MY ZIP'S CAUGHT AGAIN!
King & Waddington
Suspicious Remarks
'Time for change!'
'A real temper!'
OFFICE

SO IT IS... HERE, LET ME
KLIK

WELL... SOME INTERESTING COMMENTS THERE. VERY INTERESTING.
HOWEVER, ON WITH THIS CHURCH BURNING BUSINESS.

HELLO, LIONEL. GET ME THE HEREFORD NUMBER, PLEASE.
YES, THAT'S RIGHT: HEREFORD.

I WANT THE S.A.S.

TONIGHT ON PANORAMA, WE INTERVIEW THE PRIME MINISTER OVER THE CHURCH ARSON AFFAIR.
HAVE THE GOVERNMENT TAKEN ACTION YET?
AND HOW DO THEY ANSWER NEIL KINNOCK'S ACCUSATION THAT THE ARSONISTS ARE BEING ALLOWED TO CONTINUE DUE TO THEIR PREVIOUS POOR RELATIONS WITH THE CHURCH OF ENGLAND?
9:Holy War

THAT'S THE PHONE. I'LL GET IT.
GOOD FOR YOU, SON. GOOD FOR YOU.
GOOD EVENING, PRIME MINISTER. THANK YOU FOR JOINING US.
THANK YOU, DAVID.

HELLO?
WELL, PRIME MINISTER, IF I MAY BEGIN BY ASKING YOU FOR YOUR PERSONAL VIEWS ON THE CHURCH ATTACKS.
I THINK YOU'LL FIND I'VE ALREADY ANSWERED THAT QUESTION, DAVID.

BUT PRIME MINISTER, WE'VE ONLY JUST STARTED THE INTERVIEW... HOW COULD YOU HAVE ALREADY ANSWERED?
AH, NIGEL. DO YOU RECOGNISE MY VOICE?
YEAH. YEAH. CORNELIUS, I RECOGNISE YOU.

GOOOOD... NOW, WE'RE LAYING ON AN OPERATION TONIGHT AND TERRY IS INSISTING YOU COME ALONG.
OH, BLOODY HELL... HE'S NOT BEEN RANTING ABOUT ME BEING HIS SON AGAIN?
ER... I, UH... HRMPH! THIS IS OBVIOUSLY JUST ANOTHER EXAMPLE OF BBC BIAS. I'LL NOT BE INVOLVED IN THIS CHARADE A MOMENT LONGER.

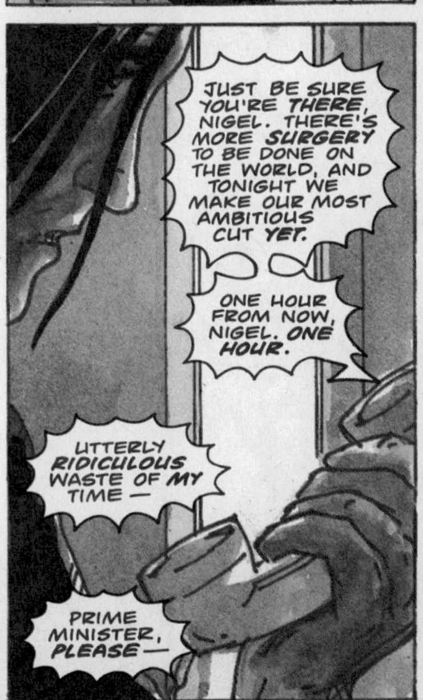
JUST BE SURE YOU'RE THERE, NIGEL. THERE'S MORE SURGERY TO BE DONE ON THE WORLD, AND TONIGHT WE MAKE OUR MOST AMBITIOUS CUT YET.
ONE HOUR FROM NOW, NIGEL. ONE HOUR.
UTTERLY RIDICULOUS WASTE OF MY TIME—
PRIME MINISTER, PLEASE—

PISS OFF, YOU WRETCHED LITTLE MAN! I SHOULDN'T HAVE TO PUT UP WITH THIS SHIT FOR THE BENEFIT OF THE PEASANTS—
PRIME MINISTER, I'D REALLY ADVISE YOU TO TAKE OFF THE MICROPHONE... OH WELL...

EVERYONE GOT THEIR TEFLON-COATED MAGNUM LOAD DUM-DUM MERCURY INLAY BULLETS?
RIGHT, THEN.

YOU ALL KNOW THE OP... WE'VE GOT UNDERCOVER MEN AT SEVERAL CHURCHES IN LONDON. SOON AS WE GET WORD FROM THEM, A RAPID RESPONSE UNIT WILL RUSH TO THE SPOT.
OUR UNIT HAS BEEN ASSIGNED TO ST. PAUL'S CATHEDRAL.

WE'VE BEEN PROMISED FULL CO-OPERATION BY THE LOCAL BILL... IN OTHER WORDS, THEY STAY OUT OF OUR BLOODY WAY.
ANY QUESTIONS?

UH, CAPTAIN, I WAS AT LOUGH GALL... WHAT ABOUT INNOCENT BYSTANDERS?

THIS IS THE S.A.S. THERE ARE NO INNOCENT BYSTANDERS, DRAKE.
STUPID QUESTION.
YEAH, STUPID.
REALLY STUPID.
YEAH.

AND FOR GOD'S SAKE, IF THEY AREN'T CARRYING GUNS WHEN WE SHOOT THEM, MAKE SURE THEY ARE WHEN IT'S OVER, EH?
ONE GIBRALTAR SPECIAL COMING UP.

WHAT'S THIS FRIGGING HEADCASE UP TO **NOW**?
"THE BIG ONE" HE SAYS. THAT'S ALL HE'LL SAY.
"THE BIG ONE."
DYNAMITE

A LOT OF USE **YOU** WERE, **ARSEHOLE**. A **LOT** OF FRIGGING **USE**.
ALL THAT BIG TALK ABOUT YOUR HOLY MISSION TO UNBLOCK THE WORLD, AND THEN YOU JUST FOLD UP FOR THAT BASTARD CORNELIUS AND LET HIM SHAFT THE PAIR OF US GOOD AND **PROPER**.

MIND YOU, YOU HAD ME ON A ROLLER COASTER RIDE TO **HELL** LONG BEFORE HE CAME ALONG, HADN'T YOU?
**BLOODYSONOFABITCHDICKBRAINSHITHEADLOONEY!!!**
**WHY?** WHY'D YOU TURN INTO THAT? WHY'D YOU FREAK OUT IN THE **FIRST** PLACE?

WHO IN GOD'S NAME **WERE** YOU, TERRY ADAIR?

PULL OVER HERE.

WELL, GENTLEMEN... I TOLD YOU WE WERE DOING THE BIG ONE TONIGHT.

BURN IT! BURN THE WHOLE PLACE TO THE GROUND!

I WANT THIS SCUMHOLE BURNT OUT!
REMEMBER— WE'RE DOCTORS! BURN! BURN!!

BUGGER ME—

SCALPEL!!

GOOD! GOOD! CUT AND BURN, MY DISCIPLES!

MADSOD LEADER FROM ANGEL, OVER. MASOD LEADER FROM ANGEL.
MADSOD HERE, ANGEL. THEY'VE HIT YOU?
AFFIRMATIVE, MADSOD. SEE YOU IN FIVE. ANGEL OUT.

THAT'S IT! THAT'S THE WAY! DYNAMITE THE SUPPORTS AND LET'S GO!

TERRY, YOU AND NIGEL RUN FOR THE VAN! GO!

THAT MIGHT PROVE DIFFICULT...

READY LADS? ONE... TWO... THREE...
YOU'RE UNDER ARREST!!

10: False Gods

GET THEM ALL! CHECK EVERYWHERE!

WE'VE BEEN AMBUSHED! THEY'RE CUTTING US TO PIECES OUT THERE!
OH SHIT, OH SHIT, OH SHIT—

SHUT UP, YOU LITTLE BASTARD!
PISS OFF! YOU GOT US INTO THIS, YOU FRIGGING HEADCASE! YOU AND YOUR BLOODY TRUTH COMMANDOS!
WORM! PATHETIC PIECE OF SHIT!

I'M NOT SURE WE CAN GET BACK UP THE PIPE, BRETHREN. I FEAR THE BLOCKAGE HAS BEEN REINFORCED.
NOT EVEN A NEW FORMULA CAN HELP US NOW.

EH?
THINGS ARE COMING TO AN END, I THINK. IT'S ALL COMING BACK UP THE PIPE...
THESE ARE THE FINAL DAYS.

LO, THE SEVEN SEATS HAVE BEEN LIFTED, AND THE SEVEN FLUSHES SOUNDED!
AND I BEHOLD A PALE HORSE: AND HIS NAME THAT SITS ON HIM IS OVERFLOW, AND HE HERALDS THE COMING OF THE BLOCKAGE!

TERRY! TERRY! FOR GOD'S SAKE SNAP OUT OF IT!
AND THE BLOCKAGE COMETH FORTH IN THE SEEPAGE OVER THE RIM, AND IT IS LIKE UNTO A GREAT AND MIGHTY 'NUMBER TWO'...

THIS ISN'T HAPPENING TO ME...

IN THE HOUSE OF COMMONS TODAY, THE PRIME MINISTER ANSWERED HER CRITICS OVER THE PANORAMA AFFAIR, WHICH HAS PROVOKED OPPOSITION ACCUSATIONS OF HER "CONTEMPT AND DISDAIN" FOR THE PUBLIC.
NIGEL GOES BACK TO SCHOOL NEXT WEEK, DOESN'T HE?
DAD

IF THE RIGHT HONOURABLE GENTLEMAN WOULD STOP AND THINK FOR A MOMENT, HE WOULD REALISE MY USE OF THE WORD "PEASANTS" WAS AFFECTIONATE, LIKE THE LOVE OF AN INDULGENT MOTHER FOR HER CHILDREN...
UM... NO, LOVE. I THINK IT'S NEXT WEEK.

ORDER! ORDER!!
OH, THAT'S RIGHT. NEXT WEEK.

WE INTERRUPT THIS BULLETIN TO BRING YOU NEWS OF YET ANOTHER ARSON ATTACK ON A CHURCH. UNCONFIRMED REPORTS HAVE BEEN RECEIVED OF A MAJOR CONFLAGRATION AT ST. PAUL'S CATHEDRAL IN CENTRAL LONDON...
I'M SURE HE'LL BE FINE ONCE HE GETS DOWN TO SOME WORK.
MMM.
DAD

THERE HAVE ALSO BEEN REPORTS, AGAIN UNCONFIRMED, OF GUNFIRE BETWEEN THE ARSONISTS AND WHAT ONE GOVERNMENT SOURCE DESCRIBED AS "AN AS YET UNIDENTIFIED SECURITY FORCE"...
IT'S NEXT WEEK HE GOES BACK, ISN'T IT?
DAD

THE SAME SOURCE WOULD NOT DENY THE POSSIBLE INVOLVEMENT OF THE SAS IN THE ACTION.
NO... NEXT WEEK, I'M PRETTY SURE.

STOP THIS SHIT, WILL YOU! PULL YOURSELF TOGETHER!
UH...

WHAT D'YOU RECKON YOUR WIFE WOULD THINK OF YOU, EH? WOULD SHE LIKE TO SEE YOU RANTING LIKE AN ARSEHOLE? WELL? WOULD SHE?
SHE DIDN'T DIE SO YOU COULD BE LIKE THIS!!

WHAT?
THAT IS... I MEAN, ER...

I NEVER TOLD YOU ABOUT MY WIFE, CORNELIUS. HOW DO YOU KNOW ABOUT MY WIFE?
LOOK. CALM DOWN—

HOW DO YOU KNOW, CORNELIUS?
PLEASE, I'M NOT—

HOW?!

I KILLED HER.

HOLD ON A MINUTE HERE. I'M LOST. WHAT D'YOU MEAN, YOU KILLED HER?

I KILLED HIS WIFE. WELL, I HAD HER KILLED, TO BE PRECISE. GOT THE DOCTOR TO BALLS UP THE BIRTH.
TERRY HAD TO LOSE HIS FAITH, YOU SEE.

NOT REALLY, NO.
WELL, YOU SEE, IF HE DIDN'T LOSE HIS FAITH, HE COULDN'T BE A TRUTH COMMANDO, COULD HE?
THAT'S HOW I GOT THEM ALL... FIND SOMEONE WHO'S UTTERLY DEVOUT, INJECT A BIT OF PERSONAL TRAGEDY TO KILL OFF THEIR FAITH, AND BINGO! INSTANT FANATIC!

THAT'S... FOR CHRIST'S SAKE... THAT'S TOTALLY BLOODY RIDICULOUS.
OF COURSE IT IS! BUT HE BELIEVED IT, DIDN'T HE? THEY ALL DID!
YOU CAN GET PEOPLE TO BELIEVE ANYTHING!

I SPARKED THAT OFF! ME! HE WAS RUNNING AROUND SHOOTING VICARS AND BURNING CHURCHES, AND ALL THE WHILE IT HAD BEEN ME!
YOU COULD WRITE IT ALL DOWN AND IN TWO THOUSAND YEARS, WHO KNOWS WHAT THEY'D BE DOING! CHRIST ALMIGHTY, THEY'D PROBABLY BUILD A RELIGION ROUND ME!!

YES... BUT... I MEAN, IF IT WAS YOU... WELL, WHY?
I NEEDED MY ARMY TO KILL GOD, OF COURSE! DON'T ASK STUPID QUESTIONS.

BUT WHY WOULD YOU WANT TO KILL GOD?

WHY? THAT BASTARD GOD KILLED MY WIFE IN THE MIDDLE OF CHILDBIRTH!
D'YOU THINK I'M GOING TO LET HIM AWAY WITH THAT?!!

AAAAAAAAAHHH!!!

WHAT THE BLOODY HELL WAS THAT?!

I'VE BEEN MAD... I'VE BEEN MAD... I'VE BEEN SO INSANE FOR SO LONG...

WELL, HOW'D YOU THINK I FEEL?
I'M STILL INSANE!

THAT'S THE LOT OF THEM, THEN.
WHO DARES WINS.

# II: Religious Liberties

HELLO, ANGELA. HOW'RE YOU?
UM... NIGEL, ARE YOU ALRIGHT?

ALRIGHT? 'COURSE I AM. WHY WOULDN'T I BE?

WELL... IT'S JUST THAT YOU, UM, DON'T LOOK TOO WELL.
FEEL FINE.
I THOUGHT YOU WERE SUSPENDED AT THE MINUTE, ANYWAY.

I AM. JUST THOUGHT I'D POP IN FOR A WHILE.
I... I SEE. THAT ISN'T VODKA, IS IT?

YUP. WANT A DROP?
NO THANK YOU, NIGEL. I DON'T THINK IT'S A VERY SMART THING TO DO.
DON'T SAY I DIDN'T OFFER.

THERE'S SOMETHING ODD ABOUT YOU TODAY, NIGEL...
ODD? WELL, YEAH. YOU WOULDN'T BELIEVE IT, ACTUALLY.

YOU JUST WOULDN'T BELIEVE IT AT ALL.

WHAT THE HELL ARE YOU DOING HERE, GIBSON? YOU'RE STILL UNDER SUSPENSION!

AND THAT'S— MY GOD. THAT'S VODKA YOU'VE GOT THERE.

RIGHT, SON. YOU'RE COMING WITH ME. WE'LL SEE WHAT THE HEADMASTER HAS TO SAY ABOUT THIS.

WHY DON'T YOU GO AND FUCK YOURSELF?

YOU'VE DONE IT NOW, GIBSON. OH YES.

IT... IT'S NOT REAL...
OH, JESUS, IT IS. OH PLEASE, GIBSON, DON'T DO IT! PLEEEEASE—

RUGBY BUGGERS

HUH... HUH... HUH...

HOLY SHIT!!

THAT'S THE WHOLE POINT, ANGELA.

FUNNY HOW IT'S ALL TURNED OUT.

THERE GOES THE FIRE ALARM. GET ALL THE KIDDIES OUT SO THE POLICE MARKSMEN CAN DO THEIR JOB.

BUT, YEAH, IT IS FUNNY HOW IT'S ALL TURNED OUT.
THOSE TWO PRATS TRYING TO GET GOD TO COME DOWN SO THEY COULD KILL HIM.

THEY WENT LOOKING FOR HIM IN ALL THE WRONG PLACES. HE'S NOT 'UP THERE'. NEVER HAS BEEN.

HE'S RIGHT DOWN HERE WITH US, MESSING UP OUR LIVES WHENEVER HE FEELS LIKE IT.
HE'S IN US.
HE IS US.

HE OUGHT TO BE, FOR GOODNESS' SAKE.

AFTER ALL...

...WE INVENTED HIM.

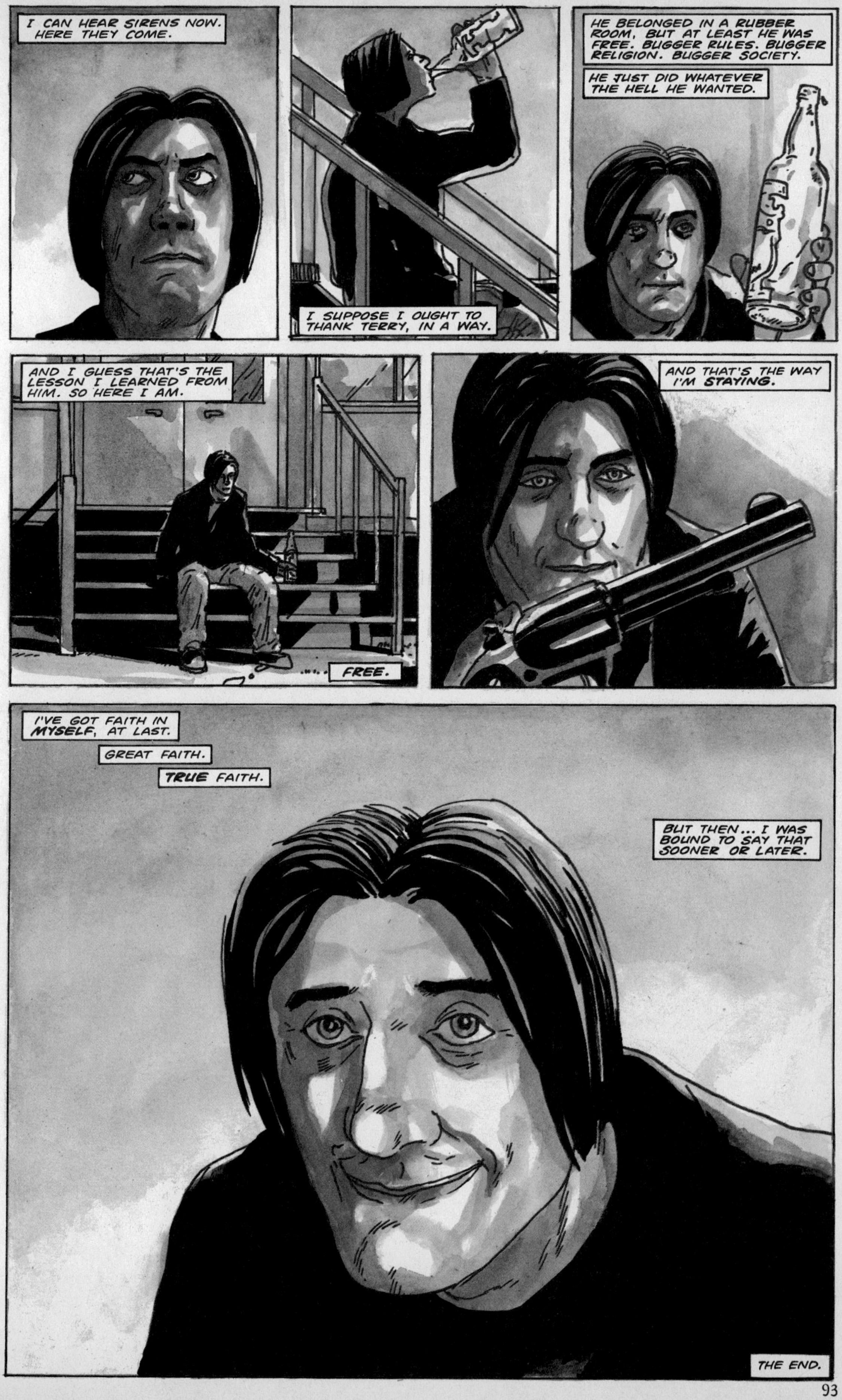

I'VE GOT FAITH IN **MYSELF**, AT LAST.

GREAT FAITH.

**TRUE** FAITH.

BUT THEN... I WAS BOUND TO SAY THAT SOONER OR LATER.

THE END.

# Biographies

GARTH ENNIS left university after three months to begin writing comics. True Faith was his second published work. A popular and acclaimed writer, his other credits include DEMON, HITMAN, HELLBLAZER, HEARTLAND, UNKNOWN SOLDIER, PRIDE & JOY, and the award-winning Preacher, which he co-created with artist Steve Dillon.

WARREN PLEECE wasted away his teenage years watching film noir. Consequently, he co-created *Velocity* with his brother Gary. Since then, his art has graced the DC/VERTIGO titles SKINGRAFT, MOBFIRE, SANDMAN MYSTERY THEATRE, HELLBLAZER and 2020 VISIONS. Other recent work includes *It's Dark In London* and *Velocity 6*. This edition features a brand-new cover painting by Pleece, who currently lives in Brighton in the south coast of England.